NIGHTMARE IN AGATE BAY

PIERCE MOSTYN PARANORMAL INVESTIGATIONS
BOOK 1

CW HAWES

CWH BOOKS

This one is for my sister, with thanks,
and
in memory of John J. "Jack" Koblas: mentor, inspiration, and friend.

JOIN THE TEAM!

Become one of my VIP Horror Readers and you'll get the latest news from my world; plus exclusive content, free stories, and other good stuff.

Begin the adventure today and you'll get a copy of *The Feeder* (not available in stores) as my thank you.

Click, tap, or scan the QR code to become a VIP Reader today!

THE PLANE WAS BEGINNING ITS FINAL DESCENT into Duluth. Special Agent in Charge Pierce Mostyn looked over the contents of the envelope he'd received that morning from Doctor Rafe Bardon, Director of the Office of Unidentified Phenomena. The letter contained the small, neat script of his boss. Complete with British spellings, even though Doctor Bardon had been in the States for over a dozen years. There was also, wafting from the paper, the faint scent of the doctor's pipe tobacco. A sweet Virginia blend.

As usual, the letter opened with a brief outline of the case, went on to include more detailed background information, plus file numbers to related cases. The second page contained the names of the members of his team for this assignment. The mission itself was simple: find out if there was any truth to the rumors regarding the inhabitants of Agate Bay, Minnesota and, if true, assess if the situation posed a threat to the security of the United States of America.

His team was comprised of two scientists, a photographer, and an additional special agent. Two of the names he was very familiar with, having worked with them before. In fact, they were assigned to him for most of his cases. Pretty much the only regular team members he had.

Mostyn re-folded the letter, slipped it into the envelope, and put the envelope in his inside suit coat pocket. He leaned back in his seat, preparing for the jolt of the jet's wheels hitting the tarmac and the braking, which always made him feel as though he was going to be propelled into the seat in front of him.

To his relief, this pilot was good. He barely felt the jet touch down, although the braking was no different than on any other flight. Mostyn had a briefcase under the seat in front of him and an overnight bag stored in the overhead compartment. The rest of his equipment was in the jet's storage hold. He was the only passenger. The jet had no markings other than its registration number and a small American flag on the tailfin.

Mostyn deplaned with his briefcase and bag. The other equipment would be taken to a nondescript building on Airpark Boulevard by OUP agents. That's also where he'd meet his team members in the evening. In the meantime, his driver would take him to a hotel.

He walked down the jetway towards the terminal. A man of averages. Average height. Average weight. Average looks. The only physical feature that could be said to be distinguishing was his short strawberry blond hair. Even so, he could still walk past most people and they'd remember nothing about him.

His suit was expensive. Dark chocolate in color. The shirt was a shade of pale blue, custom made by one of the finest tailors in the DC area. He wore a repp tie of brown and blue stripes. A very pale red handkerchief stylishly adorned the jacket's breast pocket. The outfit was one that might catch the eye of certain individuals.

Upon entering the terminal, he spotted the black-suited woman holding a card with his last name printed on it and walked over to her.

"I'm Mostyn."

"Special Agent Biyanka Patel, sir. Pleased to meet you. I'm very much looking forward to this assignment, sir. This opportunity to work with you."

Mostyn took in the fresh scrubbed face, the eagerness of a new agent to please the one in charge. "You might not think that when we're done, Patel."

"How's that, sir?"

"How long have you been with the OUP?"

"Three weeks, sir."

"Where were you before this?"

"DIA."

"Defense Intelligence Agency?"

"Yes, sir. Before that I was in Swick."

Mostyn raised his eyebrows. "A Navy Special Warfare Combatant-craft Crewman?"

"Yes, sir."

"Why did you join OUP?"

"When I was young, about twelve, I saw my grand-mother working in our garden."

"Okay."

"She'd been dead for three years, yet there she was. Just like these chairs." She waved her hand towards the rows of seats in the waiting area.

"I see. Bardon found out and recruited you."

"Yes, sir."

"Are the others here?"

"They're at their respective hotels. All except for Doctor Kemper, sir."

"Very good. Let's get on with it."

"Yes, sir."

"And Patel?"

"Yes, sir?"

"We're fairly informal on this team. Mostyn will do."

"Yes, sir. Uh, Mostyn."

He smiled and indicated she should lead the way.

Mostyn followed her out of the terminal building to the black four door sedan. She got in the driver's seat and he took the passenger's, after tossing his bags onto the backseat.

He was surprised at how warm the November day was in Duluth. He'd had visions of snow on the ground and flakes flying in the air. The temperature was in the low sixties and the sun was shining. No clouds at all in the sky. The wind, though, was gusting up to thirty miles per hour. He was glad it was not coming in off Lake Superior.

Patel started the sedan and drove out of the airport. They were at the hotel in a couple minutes.

"Where are you staying, Patel?"

"Here, sir, but on a different floor."

Mostyn smiled at her use of "sir" and nodded his head in acknowledgement of her answer. He got out of the car, retrieved his bags, and watched Patel drive out the hotel's driveway and back to the airport. He turned to the front door and checked his watch. There was plenty of time to get to his room, freshen up, and prepare for tonight's meeting.

————

The two scientists and the photographer were waiting for him when he and Patel arrived in the small meeting room. He smiled at Doctor Dotty Kemper and the photographer, Willie Lee Baker. They were the ones he'd worked with numerous times before during the past five years, since he'd accepted reassignment from the FBI to the Office of Unidentified Phenomena.

There were probably agencies more secret than the OUP, but if there were Mostyn didn't know about them. It was rumored less than fifty men and women knew of the ultra-secret office he worked for. In point of fact, Mostyn was still officially listed as an FBI agent and his pay still came from the Bureau.

He extended his hand to the person he didn't know. "Pierce Mostyn."

The thirtyish, bespectacled, and rather nerdy looking fellow took his hand and replied, "Travis Templeton. I'm your physical anthropologist."

Mostyn nodded and turned his attention to the others. "Hi, Dot, Willie Lee. Good to see you again."

Willie Lee gave him a lazy salute and said, "Mostyn."

Dotty shifted in her seat and put her hands behind her head. "So what is it this time? Space aliens living on some remote island in Superior or mutant yetis on a cannibalistic rampage in the Boundary Waters Wilderness Area?"

Mostyn chuckled and sat in an empty chair at the table. "Neither. Tomorrow morning we'll be driving up to the little town of Agate Bay. Rumors about the inhabitants have come to someone's attention, someone high up enough that they could apprise the Director of the FBI. However, Doctor Bardon learned of the rumors and claimed jurisdiction."

"Which explains why we're spending the weekend on the backend of nowhere," Dotty finished.

A hint of a smile crossed Mostyn's lips. "Something like that."

"So what's the story?" Baker asked.

Mostyn became serious. "The possibility exists of some manner of disease affecting the inhabitants. According to the rumors, it's a localized occurrence. It hasn't spread to nearby Two Harbors or down here to Duluth."

"Isn't that kind of odd?" Templeton asked.

"That's why we're here and not the CDC," Kemper said. "Someone thinks it's too odd and Bardon agrees. Which also means that what we hear isn't necessarily what we'll end up seeing."

"What does that mean?" Templeton asked.

Kemper smiled at the newbie. "I'll let the boss explain."

"Thanks, Kemper," Mostyn said. He turned to Templeton. "What the good doctor means is that we aren't often told the whole truth of the situation. Although to be fair, sometimes Bardon doesn't know the whole truth."

Kemper snorted a laugh. "Yeah, right, Mostyn. There's a bridge—"

He waved away her retort and she laughed.

Templeton shook his head at the banter and asked, "Do we have any idea of the symptoms of this supposed disease?"

"We've been told a few things," Mostyn replied. "The disease appears to be some manner of degenerative affliction. Symptoms start showing up when a person is in his or her twenties or thirties, gets progressively worse, until the person is so deformed even the locals keep him or her out of sight."

"What are the symptoms?" Kemper asked.

"Supposedly quite hideous," Mostyn answered. "The disease affects skin and bones. The skin gradually changes color to a grayish green and becomes scabrous. The hair falls out and the eyes become bulging and the person rarely, if ever, blinks. The skeleton becomes misshapen. The head elongates and the limbs become deformed to the extent that the fingers become fused together and the legs and feet are so affected a normal human gait becomes impossible."

"Sounds hideous," Patel said.

"Yes, it does," Mostyn replied.

"Probably someone in a Halloween costume," Kemper said, a hint of disgust in her voice.

"Could be," Mostyn agreed. "Although the prank would get a little old after close to a hundred and thirty years."

Kemper was undeterred. "Maybe it's something in their water."

"Maybe," Mostyn said, a smile touching his lips. He continued, "We'll find out tomorrow. Our mission is to drive to Agate Bay and talk to the people, if we can. They are reported to be suspicious of outsiders. Especially government types. Which is why we need to maintain our cover as tourists."

Patel was looking at her phone. "According to the maps," she tapped the device, "the main road bypasses Agate Bay and the town looks to be surrounded by pretty dense forest." She looked up at the group. "They can't get many tourists, cut off like that."

"Which could explain why they're suspicious of outsiders," Baker said.

"Could very well be, Willie Lee. Any questions?" Mostyn asked.

"If we're just going there to talk to people, why am I here instead of, say, a medical doctor?" Patel asked.

Mostyn thought a moment before answering, "You're here to provide protection for the civilians should they need it. Like the Boy Scouts, we're prepared. Any other questions?"

There were none, and the meeting broke up, with Patel

taking Templeton and Baker to their hotels first. When Kemper and Mostyn were alone, Kemper said, "That was a good cover, Mostyn."

"What do you mean?"

"You know what I mean. She's really here to put lead into your and Bardon's boogeymen."

2

THE MORNING SKY WAS CLEAR AND THE temperature cold. Mid-thirties, with a wind blowing right out of Canada. Patel had exchanged the sedan for a big black SUV in order to better carry the team members and their gear. The drive to Agate Bay took just under an hour.

For most of the trip, Mostyn and his team had a clear view of trees. Trees on their left, the inland side, and trees on their right, the side toward Lake Superior. Once out of Duluth, there were only occasional houses to break the monotony of the evergreens. Minnesota Route 61 was pretty much like any other four-lane highway.

At one point Templeton quipped, "I'm glad we're going in the day. At night I don't think I could see my own hand even if it were right in front of my face."

There were murmurs of agreement.

Minnesota 61 turned into a two-lane road outside of Two Harbors and the team was able to get a better view of the lake.

"Looks like the ocean," Patel said.

"I've been out there on a boat," Baker said, "and let me tell you, you really do think you're on the ocean. That is one big lake."

After several miles, the GPS announced the turn off to Agate Bay. However, Patel nearly missed it because it was not at all clearly marked. Once on the road, they discovered the pavement ceased a hundred feet from the turn and was replaced by a gravel road from which most of the gravel had disappeared. The pine, spruce, and fir trees pressed in on the nearly abandoned looking road, blotting out much of the sun, and casting an unnatural gloom.

The big SUV bumped, shimmied, and slew through the potholes and ruts. When the right front tire hit one particularly deep pothole the steering wheel was wrenched out of Patel's hands. After several colorful words which made clear her having been a sailor, the vehicle continued down the road toward their destination.

Templeton said, "There's no traffic. Don't these people go anywhere?"

"According to the notes from Bardon, there are a few businesses in Agate Bay and the owners make occasional trips to Two Harbors or Duluth," Mostyn answered. "Otherwise, the people pretty much stick to themselves."

"What kind of businesses?" Baker asked.

"I don't know," Mostyn said. "Bardon didn't elaborate."

"Probably like any other small town," Kemper said. "Ten bars to offset the five churches."

The SUV bounced through a curve in the road and Patel

stepped on the brake. Before them was the village of Agate Bay.

"The place looks like a ghost town," Patel said.

"Maybe the disease finally ate them," Kemper sneered.

And then, out of one of the dilapidated buildings, a person clumsily shambled, stopped, gazed at the vehicle for a few moments, and then shambled off down the street.

"Better luck next time, Kemper," Mostyn said.

"Instead of sitting here, maybe we can get on with it," she shot back.

Patel looked over at Mostyn, who was in the passenger seat.

"Drive on," he commanded. "Let's see if we can find an active business. Some people to talk to."

Patel guided the SUV into the village. On either side of the street were houses in all manner of disrepair; some no longer fit for human habitation, others were boarded up, and a few showed signs that people were still living in them. Curtains might be hanging in the windows or smoke might be drifting from a chimney. All of the buildings needed paint, and more than a few some manner of structural repair.

They had entered the town on 3rd Street and, aside from the lone person they'd seen, the street was strangely empty. At the corner of 3rd and Main, Patel turned left into what had probably once been the business district. Now on either hand was vacant building after vacant building. However, in the second block there was, in stark contrast to the surrounding buildings due to its newness, a small Super One grocery store.

"Park here, Patel," Mostyn ordered.

She pulled over to the curb and parked. The team piled out of the vehicle.

"The place reeks of fish," Templeton said, pinching his nose.

"Must have a processing plant here," Baker added.

"There's commercial fishing on the Great Lakes?" Kemper asked.

"Obviously, with this stench," Templeton said.

Mostyn smiled at Templeton's slam. Kemper, on the other hand, gave her fellow anthropologist the finger.

The team entered the little grocery. The only people in evidence were a man and a woman. The woman was sitting in the front of the store by one of two cash registers. She looked up from the magazine she was reading, but said nothing. The man was in one of the aisles checking the shelves. He spoke.

"Hi. May I help you?"

Templeton and Baker shook their heads. Kemper asked about the fish smell.

"It's pretty pervasive. A lot of it comes from the processing plant."

"Processing plant?" Kemper asked.

"Yeah. This is the most productive fishing spot in all of the Great Lakes. There are always fish here and in tremendous quantities. Rather odd, that, given the declining fish populations in not only the other areas of Superior, but all the lakes."

"Why do you think that is?" Kemper inquired.

The man's answer came almost too quick. "Don't rightly know. Been that way for years. Why do you ask?"

Kemper shrugged. "Curious."

"Not many people around," Mostyn said. "Thought the place was abandoned until we saw a person. Looked like he, or maybe she, had been in an accident."

The man and woman looked at each other. The man said, "You folks aren't from around here, are you?"

"No, we're not," Mostyn affirmed. "We're from Illinois visiting your state. Someone told us to visit the North Shore." Mostyn shrugged. "So here we are."

The man nodded, accepting Mostyn's story. "Yep. The North Shore is beautiful. All except this place. If there's a hell, this place has to be the vestibule."

"Why's that?" Kemper asked.

The man hesitated and the woman said, "Tell 'em."

"The godawful smell, for one," the man said. "And, for two, the people themselves. My wife and I...," he waved his arm toward the woman at the cash register, "...we're from Superior, over in Wisconsin. Took this job without quite knowing what we were getting ourselves into. But we need the money and the pay's decent. Jobs are hard to find up here and we didn't want to move to Milwaukee or Minneapolis."

The wife interrupted, "So we took the job to run this store. Awful place. Wish now we hadn't, but hindsight is twenty-twenty as they say."

"People here are peculiar," the man said. "Not at all friendly. You won't find Minnesota Nice here! I think they actually do their best to drive strangers away."

"What about you?" Templeton asked.

"Oh, they didn't want us here at first," the man explained. "Probably still don't. They mostly just ignore us now."

"Don't forget the vandalism," the woman said. "Broke a couple windows they did."

"They also dumped fish guts on our porch a couple times," the man said. "When we didn't leave, they started shunning us."

"Do they come into the store?" Patel asked.

"Rarely," the man answered. "Not sure why the owners bother to keep the place open."

"What are the people like? Besides being unfriendly," Templeton asked.

"Weird," the woman said.

"That they are," the man concurred. "Although they're pretty normal until they reach puberty. A lot of them start changing then. That's when they start stinking of fish too."

Mostyn asked, "What do you mean by 'once they begin the change'?"

The woman interrupted. "I wouldn't say 'a lot', Phil. A few of them get the disease that early. Most seem to get it in their twenties. The rest in their thirties."

"Disease?" Kemper asked, feigning fear.

"Oh, it's not anything you can catch," the man said.

"Just affects the locals," the woman added. "That's why we haven't got it."

"Anyone immune?" Kemper asked.

"None that I've seen," the woman said, adding, "If you're a local, that is."

"What's the disease like?" Templeton asked.

"Most hideous damn thing you'll ever see," the man said. "It's the change and none of them seems to be immune. It starts with the skin turning that peculiar grayish color and the hair begins to fall out. The head begins to elongate and the hands and feet begin to change. Creases develop in the neck and gradually get deeper. Remind me of gills in a fish. Then the voice starts changing, becoming hoarse and guttural and pretty disgusting to listen to. Lastly are the eyes. They turn dull and expressionless, as does the entire face, and then they gradually bulge outward. The eyes do. Eventually the person ceases to blink at all."

"But it doesn't stop there," the woman said. "They just keep getting uglier and uglier until their own people can't no longer stand the sight of them and they lock them away."

"Seems the older they get, the worse the symptoms of the disease," the man added.

"And you're sure we can't catch it?" Templeton asked.

"Nope." The man shook his head. "That's the good part. Seems to only affect those born here."

Templeton's face took on a thoughtful and far away look.

Kemper asked, "How long have you been here?"

"Year and a half," the woman replied.

"Do you have any friends—?" Baker began before he was cut off by the woman.

"With these people? Ha! I tell you we're lucky to be alive."

"Now Linda," the man said.

"It's true, Phil." She turned to Mostyn's group. "I know they leave us alone now. But I still don't trust 'em. No, sirree. Why, several locals have disappeared. Those people killed them. I know it. That priest of theirs. They worship the devil. Sacrifice people."

"Now Linda. None of that's ever been proven."

"Maybe not," she shot back, "but something weird goes on in that church of theirs."

"Any chance the locals will talk to us?" Mostyn asked.

"Not likely," Phil said. "If you find ol' Caleb, you might get him to talking. He's, what, Linda, about ninety? Ninety-five?"

She nodded.

Phil continued, "He's a drunk, but completely normal. You might get something from him."

Mostyn thanked Phil and Linda for the information and made ready to leave, when Phil spoke up again.

"I don't know how long you're staying. You might, though, want to buy something for lunch. The café in town is run by a local family and the food is none too good. Seriously. I'm not saying that just to make a sale."

Mostyn thanked him for the tip. The group bought food and drink for lunch and left. Out on the street, Dotty Kemper asked how they should proceed.

"Dotty, you, Baker, and Patel form one team. Templeton and I will form the other. Let's meet back here at four to compare notes."

Phil stepped out onto the sidewalk. "One more thing. I hope you weren't planning on staying overnight."

"We weren't," Mostyn said.

"Good. Because the Bayview Hotel doesn't have a good reputation. Not long after we arrived here a tourist went missing. Supposedly got lost in the woods. However, they never found his body. Then just a couple months ago two tourists that stayed there became completely unhinged and apparently no one was able to get anything coherent out of them. Just some babbling about monsters."

"That could describe most of the town, couldn't it?" Templeton said.

The man nodded, "Yep. I guess it could."

3

From the back of the big SUV, the team members loaded up on equipment. Baker got his camera. Patel and Mostyn picked up extra ammunition and retrieved their backup weapons, as well as pocket flashlights. Mostyn added a small pair of binoculars to his collection. Kemper and Templeton each retrieved a little recording device with which to keep a record of their observations.

Mostyn directed Kemper, Baker, and Patel to explore the north end of the village. He looked at his watch. The time was just before eleven. That gave them five hours to gather whatever information they could.

"Which way, Mostyn?" Templeton asked after the others began walking away to the north.

"Let's go down to the lake and start there. We'll work our way back to here."

Templeton nodded and the two men walked over to what turned out to be Washington Street, turned right, and began walking towards the lake. The buildings were uniformly unkempt. If there was any paint on the wooden boards, it was peeling off. The universal color seemed to be a weathered gray. Many, though, if not most, were derelicts and showing the decay that goes with a building long abandoned. Many roofs had holes in them or had fallen in completely. Windows were frequently broken and many were boarded up.

The streets themselves were in an advanced state of disrepair. Much of the asphalt was broken up and plants, even trees, were growing in the cracks and potholes. The sidewalks were no better.

"Where is everyone?" Templeton asked. "Given the size of this place, there had to be at least three or four hundred people here at one time."

Mostyn nodded. "At one time. Can't be anywhere near that number now."

Templeton recorded his observation and was putting the recorder in his pocket when he motioned with his head and said, "Just saw the curtain move in that house. Maybe we should knock on the door. Ask directions or something."

"No. Not unless we have a really good cover story that gives us a reason to do so. We need to ask ourselves, 'Is that something a tourist would do.' If the answer is 'no', we don't do it."

"Okay. You're the boss."

Washington dead-ended at Lake Street, which ran along the shoreline of Lake Superior. Paralleling Lake, just to the north, was a rail line overgrown with weeds. Standing at the corner, the two men looked left and right. In both directions they saw warehouses collapsing in on themselves and the crumbling, rotting wharf stretching up and down the shoreline. The sole exception to this depressing vista of decay was the fish factory several blocks away.

Mostyn pointed towards the factory. "Let's take a look. The processing plant seems to be the only building, aside from the grocery store, that isn't falling down or in danger of doing so."

When there was no response from Templeton, Mostyn looked at him. The anthropologist's gaze was directed towards the lake.

Mostyn smiled. "Never seen Lake Superior before?"

"No. It's huge!"

"That it is."

"I mean, look, it just goes on forever. There's no land whatsoever out there. Just water and sky."

"Yep. And when there's a storm it can be as bad as being on the ocean. Some say worse."

Templeton took out his phone and took a picture of the vast expanse of water.

"Okay, now that you've taken your bona fide tourist photo, can we focus on the mission?"

"Sure. Sorry."

Mostyn took out his binoculars and examined the building. "Well, maybe I spoke too soon."

"About what?"

"The building being in good shape. It needs work, but still looks solid."

He put the binoculars away and the two men set off for

the factory, Templeton complaining vociferously about the overpowering fish stench. And the closer they got the more he complained.

Mostyn, on the other hand, was looking all around, his pace gradually slowing until he'd stopped.

"What's the matter?" Templeton asked, he also stopping.

"Birds."

"What about them?"

"There aren't any. Which is pretty damn odd. No seagulls around a fish plant?"

"Yeah. Come to think of it, they're usually everywhere making a nuisance of themselves."

"Right. So where are they?"

"Don't know. That's kind of spooky. And now that you mention it, there hasn't been so much as a squirrel since we entered this place."

"Right."

"I mean, squirrels are everywhere. So why not here?"

"Good question, Mr. Templeton. Good question."

They started walking again and Mostyn turned his attention back to the fish plant and the activity around the place. Several villagers were clearly visible, having just come out of the building to do something on the platform that was next to the factory and projected out over the water. He pointed them out to Templeton.

The anthropologist stopped walking and stared at the villagers, asking Mostyn for his binoculars. Mostyn handed them over, and Templeton stared at the workers for some time before handing the field glasses back to Mostyn.

"They *are* hideous beings," he said. "Worse than what they were saying at the grocery store. I mean it's one thing to describe bulging eyes and the gray, scabrous skin, but it's another thing to actually see it. God, it's creepy. Just like a horror movie. Whatever this disease is, I'm glad it hasn't shown up anywhere else."

"Actually it has."

Templeton stared at Mostyn. "It has? Where? When? I've never heard of it before."

Mostyn started walking and Templeton joined him. "Innsmouth, Massachusetts. The winter of nineteen twenty-seven and twenty-eight. The Federal government received a tip regarding the strange goings on in the town. There were so many arrests and deportations, the town was effectively depopulated."

"I've never heard of this."

"I'm not surprised."

Templeton took out his phone.

Mostyn gave a little laugh. "Oh, you won't find any references to Innsmouth. All very hush-hush. The town doesn't actually exist anymore. At least for the regular old citizen of the US of A. The little I know came from a heavily redacted report I read when I first started with OUP. Not even Director Bardon knows all of it, although he has other sources at his disposal and probably knows all about it in spite of what the government refuses to tell him. That's why he took this case away from the FBI."

"Why would the government keep this disease a secret?"

Mostyn stopped and took a deep breath. "Keep this under your hat, Templeton, understand?"

He nodded.

Mostyn continued, "From what I read, the little I read because the report was so heavily redacted, mind you, the people of Innsmouth didn't suffer from any disease. And whatever it was that afflicted them, apparently is also at work here in Agate Bay."

4

TEMPLETON SWALLOWED. HE CAST A GLANCE towards the people working on the platform next to the plant. "If it..." He cleared his throat. "If it isn't a disease, then what is it? Genetic mutation?"

"You're the scientist. You tell me." Mostyn started walking again and Templeton with him.

The anthropologist walked, looking at the ground. Apparently deep in thought. In a few moments, he said, "You're sure it isn't a disease?"

Mostyn shrugged. "No. Not one hundred percent sure. And the Feds aren't sure that it isn't. But if it is, pretty odd that no one's gotten it except for the people who lived in Innsmouth and those living here in Agate Bay."

Templeton nodded. "Doesn't seem like a disease. Which means it probably is genetic and successive generations of inbreeding has brought out some nasty recessive genes, or it's caused by something in the environment. But if environmental, very odd that at two different times and two different locations the same catalyst would be present to cause the same symptoms."

"Right. Personally, I don't think the origin of these people's problem and those of Innsmouth is environmental in nature. Which leaves genetic. But what recessive gene would produce this?" With a movement of his hand, Mostyn indicated the men working outside the fish factory.

"I don't know," Templeton said. "Quite honestly, this is beyond anything in my experience."

In another minute they were at the factory. The smell of fish was overpowering. The villagers were in plain sight and it was easy to see their deformities, the hideousness of which had to at least rival those of the famous Elephant Man, if not actually surpass them. Mostyn and Templeton were getting their first close look at citizens of Agate Bay, Minnesota. And it was not a pleasant sight.

They saw for themselves the dull, expressionless faces. The narrow heads with the bulging eyes that never seemed to blink. The flat noses and the ears which seemed to have almost disappeared entirely, leaving only vestigial remains. The large-pored grayish skin, which, in places, looked to be peeling and scabrous, as if from some particularly noxious skin condition. The sight made Templeton shudder.

The village men working out on the platform walked with a peculiarly clumsy and shambling gait, undoubtedly due to their exceptionally large feet. Their hands were overly large as well, although the fingers were thick and stunted.

Templeton seemed speechless. He simply stared at them.

Mostyn called out, "Say, we're visiting the area and wondered if we might have a tour of the factory."

There was no response by the men.

Mostyn repeated the request.

One man stopped his work, looked up, and in a harshly guttural voice, his words slurred to an almost indecipherable dialect, said, "Leave. Not safe."

Mostyn and Templeton looked at each other and back to the fellow, who lifted a large, deformed hand, pointed to the north, and repeated, "Leave. Not safe."

Templeton muttered, "Holy shit."

Giving the fellow a lazy salute, Mostyn turned and started walking in the direction he and Templeton had come. The anthropologist followed and caught up.

"What needs to be done," Templeton said, "is to spend some time with these people and run tests. That's the proper way to do it."

Mostyn simply said, "Maybe. You want to do it?"

The anthropologist said nothing, until Mostyn's gaze prompted him to speech. "It's... It's the only way to find out what is actually going on here."

Mostyn stopped and looked at the lake. It went on seemingly forever, just like the ocean. He pointed. "See that low-lying rock out there in the water?"

"What of it?"

"Innsmouth had the same thing. Devil Reef they called it. It was said to be the source of all their problems."

"What do you mean?"

"Just what I said."

"Come on, Mostyn. What do you mean?" There was a tremor in Templeton's voice.

"I don't know anymore. Kind of odd, though, that Agate Bay and Innsmouth should both have a low-lying rock situated offshore."

Mostyn started walking again, with Templeton following, and, at the next cross street, he turned up the street, and at the next intersection turned west again. When he was directly north of the processing plant, he stopped. The building in front of them was falling in on itself. Mostyn got up next to the side of the place and peered around the corner, taking a long look at the fish factory.

The processing plant was a big building. If what Phil had said was true, they needed a big building to handle the large number of fish that they apparently caught. Mostyn took out his field glasses and noted the condition of the building. It needed work, that much was obvious. But since it was in a much better state than any other building except the grocery store, it was pretty obvious that the villagers were willing to give what was probably the source of their livelihood at least a modicum of attention.

Templeton, standing somewhat taller than Mostyn, also peered around the corner. "What are you looking for?"

Mostyn lowered the glasses. "Just looking."

"There are more of them now."

"Uh-huh."

Having joined the original three that had been outdoors were another four men. They were having what looked to be a very animated discussion. While Mostyn and Templeton watched, two more joined the group and after a couple minutes shambled off in the same direction Mostyn and Templeton had come from when approaching the factory.

"C'mon," Mostyn said.

The two men crossed the street and entered the yard of a house that was falling in on itself. The grass had long ago given way to a surfeit of weeds and shrub-like growth. Mostyn and Templeton made their way through the brown and brittle vegetation and walked along the side of the house, at last entering the backyard. Some one hundred feet from the house and sitting higher than it, for the terrain rose from the lakeshore in a fairly steep incline, was a small wooden building.

"I'm going to guess that's a garage," Mostyn said, and he immediately made for it. Templeton jogged after him.

"What's going on?" the anthropologist asked.

"I think they sent two of their number to follow us."

"Oh, shit. That can't be good, can it?"

"I wouldn't think so," Mostyn said, while turning the doorknob and pushing open the side door to the garage.

He stood in the doorway and took the flashlight out of his coat pocket and played the beam around the interior of the place. The grime-covered windows let in but a modicum of light. The beam of the flashlight picked up several rats, and there were cobwebs everywhere. He played the light over a workbench with a few rusting and moldering tools on it, but the thing of most interest was the ancient automobile sitting in the middle of the floor.

Mostyn entered the garage and walked around the car.

Templeton stepped through the doorway and pushed the door closed.

"Well, I'll be damned," Mostyn said.

"I don't think that's a wise choice of words."

Mostyn looked up at the young scientist. "The place getting to you?"

"Yes."

"This is nothing. So far, anyway. How long have you been with the OUP?"

"Just a couple missions."

"What were they?" Mostyn asked.

"Examined a site that may have been an ancient UFO landing field and explored a supposedly haunted cavern."

"Well, if you stay with the OUP…" He paused and then said, "Let's just say this is nothing. Yet."

Mostyn inspected the grimy old car. "A Columbia Six. This is an impressive find. Not many of these were made."

"How long are we going to stay here?" Templeton asked, his voice betraying his apprehension.

Mostyn took out his smart phone. "Great. No reception. Goddamn boondocks." He paused and then continued, "I need to get word to the others. If the villagers view us as a threat, or at least enough of a threat to put tails on us, I don't think that bodes well."

"What are we going to do?"

"Let's get back to the SUV. You can stay there, while I find the others. Depending on what they've found, we'll decide what's next."

"Do I have to stay by myself? I mean, seriously, this place is giving me the creeps bad."

"You'll be okay, Templeton. I doubt they'll try anything in broad daylight."

Mostyn opened the door a crack and peered out. He crouched down and exited the garage, holding up his hand indicating Templeton should stay put. He moved to the alley, looked up and down the length of it, and then motioned for his partner to follow.

The alley was weed choked and the men proceeded with some difficulty over the broken and crumbling asphalt. When they came out onto the street, they turned north.

"That house there, Mostyn, the curtain just moved."

Pierce Mostyn followed the pointing finger of his partner. "I wonder if they have a phone tree in operation to keep tabs on strangers?" he mused.

"Maybe. The women in my grandmother's church were all on one. More effective than social media."

"No doubt."

"Uh, that's not a good thing. Is it?"

"For us? Probably not."

The two men made their way through the deteriorating streets in the direction of the grocery store and the SUV, their progress marked by subtly moving curtains all along the way.

"Maybe we should run," Templeton suggested.

"No. We're just tourists. We can't let them think we're anything else."

"This place is creeping me out big time."

"Don't let it. Just focus on getting back to our vehicle."

They continued walking at a leisurely pace. Twice Mostyn caught glimpses of shambling-gaited figures ducking into the dark recesses of crumbling houses. He pretended he didn't see them and walked on, making idle chit-chat with Templeton.

They reached the SUV by quarter to one. The store was closed.

"Don't you think it odd the store would close in the middle of the day?" Templeton asked.

Mostyn shrugged. "This isn't the big city. Maybe there's no good business reason to be open past noon." He tried the driver's door. It opened. "Good. Patel left the door open. Get in and wait here. Lock the doors if you want. I'm going to find the others. Should be back soon."

"Good luck."

Mostyn nodded and took off at a leisurely pace, conscious of the watery, unblinking eyes watching him from behind curtained windows.

5

MOSTYN WALKED DOWN THE STREET TO ADAMS and turned north. He took in the decaying architecture. Most of the buildings were in a late Victorian style, with a crumbling Romanesque appearing here and there. In their day, they would have been grand homes. Once out of sight of the store, he picked up his pace. On reaching the first cross street, he paused and looked first right and then left. He didn't see the other members of his team.

At the next block he again looked up and down the street. Deserted like the others. He turned around. Most of the village stretched out before him down to the shore of Lake Superior. The east-west streets gave the place a terraced look. From where he was standing he saw the fish factory rising above the surrounding darkly dilapidated and rotting structures. And further out, about half a mile off shore, was the rock; rising no more than a few feet above the waves.

Mostyn murmured, "So like Innsmouth," and then

moved on up the hill to the next cross street. There were no street signs in this part of town. Time and weather must've taken them. He also noticed how the forest was beginning to encroach on the nearly abandoned village.

He looked up and down the cross street and there they were, maybe four blocks away. He whistled and waved to get their attention. In the unnatural quiet, the whistle sounded loud and shrill.

Dotty Kemper waved back. Mostyn trotted towards his team members and they began walking in his direction. When they met up, Mostyn asked if they'd run into any trouble.

Kemper answered. "No trouble. Haven't really seen anyone."

Patel interrupted. "We're being watched. Lots of furtive movements behind curtained windows."

Mostyn nodded.

Kemper continued, "We did catch a glimpse of something that might prove to be of significant interest."

"Unfortunately, I couldn't get a picture," Baker said. "It all happened so fast."

"What was it?" Mostyn asked.

"Nothing 'happened'," Kemper corrected. "We were over on the other side of town and saw a building."

Baker continued. "Probably a church at some point in the past. Looked like an old church would look. Just no crosses or crucifixes."

Kemper shot him a perturbed look.

"What?" he replied. "Pissed that I added some data?"

Kemper ignored him and went on, "A sign outside gave

the name as 'The Reorganized Esoteric Order of Dagon'. What is it, Mostyn?"

At hearing the name of the building, Mostyn had blanched. He regained his composure and then explained.

"Some ninety years ago the Federal government raided the town of Innsmouth, Massachusetts. The main church, maybe religious cult would be a better description, was the Esoteric Order of Dagon. Very little is known about the group. Aside from incidental and non-important papers, the order wrote nothing down. Their beliefs and practices were maintained by oral tradition and are virtually unknown to this day. Very little information was gotten out of the inhabitants the government took into custody."

Kemper's eyes lit up. "So are you saying this group is the same as that group?"

"I'm not saying anything. I'm pointing out a coincidence."

Kemper laughed. "Come on, Mostyn. I know you well enough to know you don't put much, if any, stock in coincidences."

"Where is this place?" Mostyn asked.

"About five blocks from here," Patel answered.

"Where's Templeton?" Kemper asked.

"I left him in the vehicle. We were at the processing plant and...," he paused a moment before continuing. "We were *advised* to leave town."

"Really?" Kemper said.

Mostyn nodded, then asked, "What did you see at the church building?"

Patel answered, "The door was open, so we decided to go in and look around."

"To see if we could find any clues as to what's going on," Baker added.

Kemper continued the narrative, "The building had obviously been a church at some point in the past. Pulpit, altar railing, even an old organ. The pews, though, had been removed."

Patel interrupted. "We were standing just inside the front doors. The windows were dirty with dust and grime and the light wasn't good. At the front of the church were two open doors, one on either side of the choir area behind the pulpit."

"That's when we saw it," Kemper said.

Patel's olive skin was virtually drained of color. "It was hideous, sir, hideous beyond description."

Kemper cast her a look of annoyance. "We briefly — and I mean briefly — saw a figure in a black robe. I have to admit my initial impression was that the shape of the robe indicated a very peculiar body shape beneath it."

Baker picked up the narrative. "It was wearing a tiara, but it's head couldn't have been human. More like some kind of giant toad."

"Oh, for God's sake!" Kemper exclaimed. "It was misshapen, that's for sure. But a *toad*? Get a grip, Willie Lee."

Patel quietly, almost to herself, said, "Yes, a toad."

At the same time, Baker shouted, "I know what I saw, Kemper! It was like a goddamn toad!"

"It was dark in there!" Kemper's voice was filled with

anger. "Get a grip, you two. We could hardly see anything clearly."

Patel looked in shock. "A person changing into a toad." Then somewhat wild-eyed, she said in a louder voice, "What's going on here?"

Kemper shook her head. "Oh, for God's sake."

"All right," Mostyn said. "You all saw something. And...?"

"It was gone, " Kemper said. "The person saw us and fled."

"Did you pursue the person?" Mostyn asked.

"No," Kemper said. "We're supposed to be tourists. So we let it go."

Mostyn nodded. He was thoughtful for a moment before speaking. "Did you get a picture of the building, Baker?"

"I did."

"I'd like to see this place for myself," Mostyn said.

"Do we have to, sir?" Patel asked, her voice containing a silent plea.

"Get a grip, Patel. And you can cut with the 'sir'."

"Yes, sir, uh, Mostyn. Sorry. It's my training, sir. Sorry."

Kemper chuckled and even Mostyn had a smile on his face.

"Okay, Patel. Whatever makes you feel comfortable."

"Thank you, sir."

"Now, I want to see this place for myself. So let's get going. I don't want to leave Templeton alone too long. He's nervous enough as it is. Seems like this place is getting on all our nerves."

"Not mine," Kemper said.

"Of course, not you, Dot," Mostyn replied. She gave him the finger in response.

Patel took off walking in the direction of the former church building. Kemper and Baker followed, with Mostyn forming a rearguard, his eyes sweeping the dilapidated houses for any signs of life. And in the upper story of one old Victorian home, he caught a glimpse of a face. The bulging eyes and peculiar shape of the head gave the distinct impression he was looking at a man-sized toad.

———

The church was indeed nothing special. As with the fish plant, the building showed signs of some attempts to maintain a state of repair. Once upon a time it had been painted white, for flakes of the old paint still clung to the gray, weathered boards in spots. A simple one floor affair, with wings at the back to form the shape of a cross.

The double front doors were closed and, when Mostyn tried them, he found them to be locked.

"I guess they don't want any visitors," Kemper said.

He walked around the building. The windows, though covered with dirt and grime, were intact. There was a door in both of the wings and one at the back of the church and all three were locked. On the north side of the building was an entrance to the basement. The ground-level double doors were locked.

"It appears they won't make the same mistake twice," Kemper said.

Mostyn nodded his head in agreement. "Apparently. Let's get back to our ride."

The team walked southwest on 6th street and when they reached Main turned south toward the store. They hadn't proceeded more than a dozen steps when they became aware something was incredibly wrong. And even though Mostyn and his team were a block and a half away, the lack of vehicles anywhere in Agate Bay made what they saw or rather didn't see that much more obvious.

It was Patel who put their surprise into words. "Our wheels! They're gone!"

6

"WHERE'S TEMPLETON?" KEMPER SAID, HER VOICE betraying a touch of fear for the first time.

"He was with the SUV," Mostyn replied. "Come on!" he shouted, and took off running down the street. The others followed, matching his pace.

Mostyn got to the store first. The big black Ford was nowhere to be seen and the only thing that indicated it had been there was the broken window glass on the pavement.

Patel pointed to the glass. "That can't be good, sir."

"No, it can't. And I made him stay with the car." Mostyn hung his head for a moment, lifted it, and looked around. He yelled Templeton's name.

Patel, Baker, and Kemper took up the cry, but after just a few moments Mostyn motioned for them to stop.

"This isn't going to get us anywhere," he said. "We need to find a phone."

"Tell me about it," Kemper said. "I can't believe they have no cell phone reception here."

"This is the boondocks," Mostyn said.

"Tell me about it," Dotty replied.

"Let's see if we can find a pay phone, or the cafe the store owner spoke of, or the Bayview. Or any other place of business for that matter. Just something that might have a phone we can use."

"If we split up—"

"No, Patel," Mostyn interrupted. "We're going to stay together. This isn't a movie."

"And you know what happens every time they split up in a movie," Baker quipped.

"Nothing good," Kemper said.

"Enough, you two," Mostyn reprimanded. "We'll go down to 4th and walk around the block. We'll cover every block, if we have to until we find ourselves a landline. Let's get going."

They walked down to 4th Street and turned east. Vacant store fronts in crumbling buildings stared at them. Baker took a couple snapshots; the sound of the shutter, like their footsteps, was loud against the silence of the village. At Washington, they turned north. The opposite direction Mostyn and Templeton had taken just a few hours earlier. There, mid-block, they found a hardware store and a liquor store. Both were open.

"Patel, Baker, see if the hardware has a phone we can use. Kemper and I will try the liquor store. And Patel?"

"Yes, sir?"

"Don't hesitate to use your firearm."

"I won't."

Patel and Baker entered the store and when the door

closed behind them, Mostyn and Kemper went into the bottle shop.

The shelves weren't particularly well-stocked. Cheap wine, both table and fortified, cheap American blended whisky, gin, bourbon, and beer were clustered together on a few shelves, leaving most of the shelf space empty.

To their left was a counter, cash register, and clerk. A young woman, somewhere in her twenties. She was sitting on a stool and looked up when they came in. Her blonde hair was in patches, her ears smallish, and her skin scabrous and grayish hued. Her eyes had not yet begun to change, although lines were forming on her neck.

"Excuse me," Mostyn said. "Do you have a phone we can use?"

Kemper added, "Our friend and our car are missing. We want to call him."

The young woman just stared at them and then slowly began shaking her head.

"There's no phone here at all?" Mostyn pressed.

A smile spread across her thickening, grayish lips. "No phone." Her voice was harsh and guttural sounding.

"Right," Kemper said. "And my mother is from Mars."

The woman focused on Kemper and the smile disappeared. Slowly she said, her pacing staccato, "No. Phone. For. You." And then broke into a rasping, croaking cackle.

Mostyn and Kemper left the store. Patel and Baker were waiting for them.

"Any luck?" Mostyn asked.

"No," Patel answered.

Baker added, "The guy in there didn't say a word. Just

stared at us with those unblinking eyes and that damned dull expression and slowly shook his head."

"At least yours didn't say anything," Kemper said. "Ours was a loon."

"Let's keep moving," Mostyn urged.

They walked up to 5th, turned left, and walked down the abandoned block. After crossing Main, they continued to the next street, Bay, and turned left again. There, halfway down the block they found the Bayview Hotel. A large three-story Italianate-styled structure, which, like the church and the fish factory, showed some attempt at maintenance.

The hotel was separated from the other buildings on either side by a walk and strip of lawn that led around to the back of the building. The lawn showed little grass and was largely a tangle of weeds. The concrete walks showed the damage of too many harsh winters with many sections heaved up and left at an angle. The front lawn, small though it was and full of weeds, had at least been cut somewhat recently.

"Come on," Mostyn said. He mounted the short flight of steps to the covered porch, opened the door, and entered. His team right behind him.

The lobby smelled musty and was dimly lit. The team followed their leader to the registration desk.

The clerk was an older man. He had something of the Agate Bay look about him and emitted a slight fishy odor. Aside from the two people at the grocery store, he was the most normal looking native Agate Bayer any of them had seen.

Mostyn got right to the point. "I need to make a call and there's no cell phone reception. May I use your phone?"

"Guests only," the clerk replied.

"Would you make an exception?" Mostyn pulled out his wallet, extracted a fifty dollar bill and laid it on the counter.

The clerk didn't even look at it. "Guests only."

"Fine. How much for two double rooms?"

"Mostyn, we aren't going to stay here. Are we?" Patel asked, a tremor in her voice.

He turned to her. "Do you want to be on the streets after dark? I have no idea how soon help will arrive." He turned back to the clerk. "How much?"

The clerk looked down at the bill on the desk, took it, turned to the pigeon holes behind him, and turned back, placing two sets of keys on the counter.

"Now the phone."

The clerk pointed across the lobby. Mostyn followed his hand and saw an alcove with a small desk and a chair in it. He walked over to it, sat, and picked up the receiver. In a moment he was back.

"It's not working."

"Storm knocked out line. Phone company hasn't repaired."

Mostyn eyed the man for a moment and the fellow took a step back from the counter.

"Good idea, pal."

He stared at the man, moved right up to the counter, and leaned over. The man stepped back until the pigeon holes prevented any further retreat. Mostyn swept up the keys and marched to the elevator. The team piled in and they ascended to the third floor, where the door opened onto a dark hallway. The musty smell of decay assaulted them, Kemper complained about the headache she was going to get if she had to stay in the place overnight.

"I think we're stuck here, Kemper," Mostyn said, "unless you plan on walking back to Two Harbors in the dark."

Kemper gave him one of those looks intended to kill, but Mostyn was already walking down the hall to their rooms and didn't see it.

The others followed him and a disgusted Kemper brought up the rear. Down the corridor they went and at the end they found their rooms, next to each other, and by the bathroom, which was at the very end of the hallway.

Kemper walked over to the bathroom and flipped the light switch on. "What the hell is this?"

"It's a bathroom, Dotty," Baker said.

"I know that," she shot back. "I can read." She pointed to the sign on the door. "Does this mean we don't have running water in our rooms?"

"Probably," Mostyn answered.

"Oh, for the love of God." Kemper rolled her eyes and shook her head. "This is it. I'm telling Bardon to find someone else. I'm sick of this."

A smile touched the corner of Mostyn's mouth. "Maybe the Defense Department will take you. You do enough complaining for all the soldiers and sailors combined."

Patel failed to suppress a snigger.

Kemper flipped Mostyn and Patel the bird. "Come on, Mostyn, unlock the doors already."

He looked at the keys and tossed one set to Kemper. "That room's yours. Closest to the bathroom."

"Is that some kind of sexist comment, Mostyn?"

"Only if you think so, Dotty," he replied, unlocking his door and pushing it open. He turned on the light and walked in. Baker followed.

The room was plain. Dark wood, dark curtains, wallpaper in beige and dark green, peeling in spots. There was a dresser, a wardrobe, and a table with a ewer sitting inside a large bowl. There was a single, double bed.

Baker chuckled. "I guess a double room means we get cozy."

"I guess," Mostyn replied, his eyes taking in every aspect of the room.

He walked over to a door next to the wardrobe and opened it, pulling it towards him into the room. "Connecting door," he said out loud, more to himself than Baker. He tried the other door and it opened into Kemper's and Patel's room. Dotty Kemper was standing looking at the bed, balled fists resting on her hips.

Mostyn chuckled. "I hope you two keep it down in here so Baker and I can get some sleep."

Kemper pointed to the door, her face rivaling a harpy's with malevolence.

Patel was trying to suppress a smile and not doing so well.

"Get the hell out, Mostyn," Kemper spat.

7

MOSTYN LAUGHED. "FOLLOW ME, YOU TWO. TEAM meeting."

He went back through the connecting doors, the women following him into the room.

Baker had pulled open the curtains to let some natural light in.

"All right, people," Mostyn began, "we need a course of action. None of us are dressed for extended hiking in this weather. And it will be dark in another hour or so. I suggest we find a phone."

"You've been saying that, Mostyn, for some time now," Dotty said through clenched teeth.

"There's the grocery store and the people who work there," Patel volunteered.

"I think the store is the best bet," Mostyn said. "Given the attitude of the Agate Bayers, they might not like Phil and Linda helping us and take some action against them.

So I don't want to get them involved. Besides, trying to find their house is going to take too much time."

"So you're going to break into the store?" Kemper asked.

"Yes. Any other ideas?" Mostyn queried.

"Sounds like a plan," Baker said.

Patel shrugged.

"Okay. Let's go. Patel, you know how to set the door to tell if anyone's entered in our absence?"

"Yes, sir."

"Good," Mostyn replied. "Go prepare your door. We'll meet in the hall."

Mostyn tore off a small strip of wallpaper and positioned it near the bottom of the door. Hopefully an intruder wouldn't see it. There wasn't much else he could do. As an added precaution, he measured the protruding end so it was the width of his left little fingernail. That way if an intruder did see it, the odds of him or her replacing it exactly would be highly unlikely.

Mostyn led the group down the hall, but rather than take the elevator, he took the stairs. Down they went to the ground floor and out into the lobby. The clerk was sitting behind the check-in desk and watched them leave.

Once on the street, they walked north to 5th, turned right, proceeded to Main, turned right again, and made their way to the grocery store. The air was still and the sky clear. The early winter chill penetrated their coats and numbed gloveless fingers. Daylight was fading fast.

Mostyn looked over the front door. "What do you think, Patel? Alarm?"

She looked closely. "I don't think so."

He nodded. Even though the store building was new, it had been sandwiched between two other buildings, which were in an advanced state of decay. Walking to the building to the south, Mostyn tried the door and it opened on protesting hinges.

"Come on," he said. "We're going to cut through here to the alley."

They entered the dark building. Mostyn and Patel produced flashlights, which dispelled enough of the darkness so the group didn't stumble over the debris littering the floor. Rats, when caught in the light, ran squealing for the darkness.

The place had once been a women's clothier. Most of the outfits had long since rotted away into moldering piles of shapeless vermin nests. The few that remained revealed a fashion that went out of style sometime prior to the First World War.

Mostyn and his group pushed through the main display, passed the deteriorating dressing rooms and lounge area, with its rotting sofas and chairs, and into the back storage area, which was a jumble of shelving that had rotted and dumped its wares onto the floor and hanging racks that no longer held the rotting fabric that lay in piles underneath the hangers.

At the back wall, Mostyn and Patel played their flashlight beams along the bricks, from which the paint was chipping and peeling off. Patel found the door behind a pile of boxes. Mostyn and Baker cleared the way, unbarred the door, and entered the alley with the women right behind them.

A single lightbulb, in a metal bowl-shaped base with a metal cage around the bulb, cast a dull yellowish puddle of light around the door to the grocery store next door.

"How odd that they'd have a light on here and not one in the store or over the front door," Patel noted.

"One of you going to pick the lock, or are we going to freeze our butts off out here?" Kemper complained.

The door was steel with a deadbolt. It opened out into the alley.

Mostyn looked at Kemper and then tried the door. It didn't budge. "I don't have a lock pick set on me. You, Patel?"

"No, sir."

"Without something to force the lock or take the hinges apart, we aren't getting in this way," Mostyn said.

Kemper reached underneath her coat and behind her. When her hand came back to the front, a pistol was in it.

Mostyn shook his head. "You aren't shooting the lock. A ricochet could hit you or one of us. Not to mention the sound it will make. We'll go back around to the front and break the window."

"You're a spoilsport, Mostyn. You know that?" Kemper said.

"Fine. You stay here and shoot your own ass off — after we leave. And deal with the local citizenry when they come running," he replied.

Muttering something incomprehensible, Kemper put her pistol away and followed Mostyn and the others back into the abandoned clothier. But when they reached the front of the old shop, a surprise was waiting for them. Across the street they saw, in the waning daylight, three Agate Bayers, one in each of the three doorways, across from the store.

"That can't be good, sir."

"No, Patel, it isn't," Mostyn replied.

The cough made every one of them jump. Mostyn and Patel, guns drawn, played their flashlights in the direction of the sound. There, buried in a pile of moldering and disintegrating clothing, was a person, arm thrown over his eyes to protect them from the bright flashlight beams.

"Who are you?" Patel demanded.

The arm came partway down. "Caleb Peterson. You ain't gonna shoot me, are ya? I only came in here ta get some sleep. Didn't mean ta trespass or nothin'. Didn't know anyone still owned this dump. Thought they all was dead. Or gone over ta the Deep Ones."

Mostyn jumped on his comment. "Did you say 'Deep Ones'?"

"I did."

Mostyn and Patel lowered their flashlights and without the light in his eyes, Caleb Peterson lowered his arm and looked them over.

"You folks is strangers, ain't ya?"

"Yes," Mostyn said. "Do you know of the Deep Ones?"

"Can't live in Agate Bay and not know o' the Deep Ones. No sirree Bob."

Mostyn hunkered down next to the man. "What can you tell me of them?"

"I can tell you all about 'em, but I sure could use a drink ta wet my whistle. My throat's mighty dry, it is."

"We don't have a bottle and the store is being watched," Mostyn said.

"They's always a watchin' strangers. Don't like 'em. Hope you folks ain't stayin' in the hotel. Not good for a stranger's health, that place."

"What do you mean?" Patel asked.

"Sure am thirsty. Could use a drink."

"We can't get into the store," Mostyn explained again, "it's being watched. The front door."

"The store? Next door?"

Mostyn nodded.

"Aw, hell, they don't sell nothin' potable like. Gotta go ta the liquor store."

"For God's sake, Mostyn, what do you want with this old coot?"

"Look, Kemper, didn't the store people say Caleb could tell us what's happened here?"

"Him? He couldn't tell us the time of day with a clock staring him in the face."

"Could too," Caleb protested. "I may be old and a drunk, but I know all about them things and what's been goin' on here since they came. I never gave in. Never took one o' them horrors ta wife. Nope, I didn't. Cost me, but I didn't."

"Patel, Kemper, you two are armed. Go out the back and pick up a couple bottles from the liquor store. If you encounter any trouble, defend yourselves. Understood?"

"Yes, sir," Patel answered.

Dotty barked a grim laugh. "No problem on that score, Mostyn. I'd love to put a little lead into these weirdos. Even things up for Templeton."

"Nothing crazy, Dotty."

"Me? Do something crazy? I'm a doctor of forensic anthropology. I don't do crazy. We'll get the booze and be back in a flash."

The two women left. And Mostyn turned back to old Caleb.

"We'll get you something so you can quench your thirst. How long have you lived here?"

Caleb looked at him. "You ain't tourists."

"What makes you say that?"

"Cuz tourists don't pack no guns, that's why. You guvmint?"

"Yes, we're with the government," Mostyn affirmed.

"You gonna clean out this nest o' vipers?"

"Depends on what you can tell me about the disease."

"Disease?" Caleb broke out into peals of laughter. When he finally settled down, he shook his head and chuckled. "Disease? Is that what you think's goin' on here? You guvmint folks is livin' up ta your reputation."

"How's that?"

"Damn dumb. That ain't no disease those people got. God, sure am thirsty. You gettin' me a drink? My throat's parched."

"We're getting you something to drink, Caleb. Just takes a little time. That's all. So it's not a disease at work here?"

"Not the kind you folks is thinkin' of. No germs, or

bacteria, or viruses, or anything like that. No sirree Bob. Nothin' like that at work here." When he'd finished speaking he looked around, put one hand next to his mouth, and motioned for Mostyn to come closer. When he complied, Caleb whispered, "It's the work o' the devil. That's what it is. The work o' the goddamn devil."

"So what exactly is going on here?" Mostyn asked, and waved for Baker to join him.

"Who's this young fella? Say, I never got your name either. I done give you mine. Not polite not ta give me yours."

"Sorry," Mostyn said. "This is Willie Lee Baker and I'm Pierce Mostyn."

Caleb stuck out his hand and the two men shook it in turn. "Pleasure ta meet ya both."

Introductions over, Mostyn pressed Caleb for an answer to his previous question. "So what work of the devil is going on here?"

At that moment, Kemper and Patel returned. Each one had a bottle.

"Any trouble?" Mostyn asked them.

"The clerk didn't want to sell to us," Patel said.

"So I persuaded him by demonstrating he'd get a thirty-eight in his brain if he didn't," Kemper added. She turned to Caleb. "Got you whisky and…" She held up a big jug of Muscatel, "…wine. Take your pick."

Mostyn interrupted, "That, by the way, is Dotty Kemper, and this is Biyanka Patel."

"Please ta meet ya. The whisky. I'll take the whisky,

thank you. Wine is fine, but liquor's quicker." He laughed merrily at his own joke.

Patel gave him the whisky bottle and, to Kemper, mouthed, "Told you."

Kemper set down the jug of wine and gave Patel the finger.

Caleb grabbed the bottle, unscrewed the cap, and took a long pull. Afterwards, he wiped his mouth with the back of his hand and held out the bottle to the others. When no one accepted, he took another long pull. When done, he screwed the cap back on.

"Mr. Peterson, you were going to tell me what devil's work was going on here," Mostyn quietly said.

Suddenly Caleb Peterson became wary. "Why do ya want ta know?"

"I need to determine if what's going on here poses a threat to the security of America."

The old man burst out laughing. A high insane-sounding cackle. "America?" he wheezed. "Those monsters are a threat ta the universe! Ta God Hisself!"

8

"HE'S CRAZY," KEMPER BLURTED.

"Crazy, am I? You, young lady, hasn't seen *them*. The Deep Ones. Have ya?" He paused and when Kemper didn't reply, he said, "I thought so. But I have. And I'm here ta tell ya they are a spawn worse than the devil. Those hideous, bloated and croaking monstrosities... Well, no *sane* living being should have ta endure the sight o' them." He unscrewed the cap of the whisky bottle and took a long pull. And a second.

Mostyn's voice was soft. "How did they get here?"

Caleb took another pull on the bottle. "Brinnell. Alfred Brinnell. He was some shirttail relative of Obed Marsh of Innsmouth, Massachusetts. Came here in eighteen eighty. A little afore my time, seein' as I was born in twenty-two. I was the last o' the normal ones. By the time I was born the mixin' was in full swing — those monsters wantin' ta eliminate the entire human race with their noxious seed."

He took another pull on the bottle and screwed the cap back on.

"Mr. Peterson, how did they get here. The Deep Ones." Mostyn's voice was soft and gentle.

Peterson looked at him. "You believe. Doncha?"

Mostyn nodded.

"Well, as I said, it was Brinnell. He'd had hisself a fallin' out with ol' Obed Marsh and was kicked out o' Innsmouth. Eventually ended up here on the North Shore, the backside o' nowhere. Times was hard then. Food wasn't always so plentiful. Brinnell told 'em, the folks livin' here, he knew a way ta make Agate Bay prosperous. Back then it wasn't even a proper town. Just a cluster of shacks and shanties. Folks was poorer than dirt. They swallowed his story hook, line, and sinker. Yes sirree Bob. Just had ta start worshippin' that devil, Dagon. That's all they needed ta do.

"And folks here said, 'Why not? The Christian God was worthless. He didn't give nothin' but cold, snow, and starvation. So's they started worshippin' that Dagon. Brinnell showed 'em all the secret rites he'd learned o' the original Esoteric Order o' Dagon, 'cept he called his group the Reorganized Esoteric Order o' Dagon ta emphasize he was the leader.

"Well, they took a young woman and a young man and offered them ta those devils out on Disaster Rock. And they did that several more times and nothin' happened and the folks was gettin' ready ta turn on ol' Brinnell when the first o' the Deep Ones showed up. That saved Brinnell's bacon, it did, 'cuz the Deep Ones they know'd he was their ticket ta spreadin' their vile filth and they sent fish by the tens o' thousands ta our little bay. So many we couldna count 'em all. Not only were we never hungry, but there was enough for us ta start an industry and soon Agate Bay fish was bein' sold all over Minnesota and up into Canada and money was a pourin' into our little village as if we'd struck gold."

Peterson unscrewed the cap of the whisky bottle and took two long pulls, wiping his mouth with the back of his hand.

"Yes sirree Bob. We had food and we had money. Brinnell got the railroad ta put a line into town so's we could ship fish out in ice cars. Perch, salmon, whitefish, eel, smelt, and herring. Agate Bay was the fish capital o' the Great Lakes. Freighters began docking here ta haul the fish away. And there was always more. We never ran out.

"But all that success had a price, yes sirree Bob. Brinnell was the first. He took one o' those alien beings as his wife. The thing gave him twelve children. After that it was Ole Svenson who took a wife from those monstrosities. And then Gunter Hanson and his wife Helga were forced ta take mating partners from those things. Helga had eight children from her various partners and who knows how many Gunter sired. When their human daughter was old enough, she was married off ta one o' them things.

"My parents were one o' the last newcomers. My father was with the railroad. After I was born, old man Brinnell told my parents they was ta sacrifice me ta the Deep Ones and my father not only said, "no", he gave Brinnell the business end of his shotgun. That was none too good, for a mob took hold a my pa and took him out in a boat ta the Rock and threw him overboard. The monsters took him. I never knew him. Or my ma, cuz they made her mate with one o' those hideously deformed beasts and when she was done she took the meat cleaver and whacked the thing's head off and then cut off her own hand so's she'd bleed out and she did."

Old Caleb stopped there. He seemed lost in thought.

Kemper, her voice soft, asked, "What happened to you?"

Caleb eyed her. "You don't believe. Well, you stay here long enough and you will. Helga and Gunter's daughter took me in. She never did believe, even though she had ta marry one o' those things. Most o' her children with that thing died. I have a feelin' she helped that wicked spawn she was forced to birth on ta an early rendezvous with hell. No proof. Just a feelin'. She treated me like her own. She's the one who told me about my parents."

"So why do you stay here?" Patel asked.

"I have no choice. I was in the navy during the war and I thought about not comin' back, but my stepmother was ill and I came back for her. After all she'd done for me, I couldna leave her. After she died, they wouldn't let me leave. I know'd too much and they couldn't have me blabbin' ta just anybody."

"How can these 'monsters' have children with us?" Kemper asked.

Peterson laughed. "Well, missy, that's simple. It's called mating."

"Yes, I know *that*," Kemper shot back. "I mean, they aren't human. Or are they?"

"Oh, they's not so different from us as you'd think. Don't those fancy pants scientists say we all came from fish? That everything came from fish? I read once that even humans have gills when they's in the womb."

Kemper slowly nodded. "So what happens to these hybrids?"

"If they don't kill themselves, they go ta the lake and join the Deep Ones in their city in the bottom o' the lake or in the ocean off Innsmouth. Before that they change and pretty much end up lookin' like the monsters themselves. Hideous things keepin' ta their houses until they decide ta take ta the water."

He took another pull on the bottle and then another. When Peterson didn't say anymore, Kemper muttered something about a delirious drunk. Peterson heard it, jumped up, and threw the bottle across the large room where it smashed against the opposite wall.

"Fool!" he screamed. "Pray ta God ya don't see a shoggoth tonight, cuz they's a comin' for ya. All o' ya. And you're damned fools if ya stay."

Peterson saw the jug of Muscatel on the floor, snatched it up, screamed, "Fools!", once more and lurched out the front door of the ruined clothier.

Kemper repeated, this time out loud, "A delirious old drunk."

"Don't be so sure," Mostyn cautioned.

"You can't be serious," Kemper replied.

"There are three men watching this place," Mostyn said.

"We can't see them now because it's dark. But I'd bet my new fishing boat, they're there."

"What are we going to do?" Patel asked.

"Go up to the roof and try to make our escape that way," Mostyn replied.

The window shattered and a Molotov Cocktail burst on the floor.

9

Kemper let fly with an expletive and Mostyn yelled the word "stairs". Baker tried to beat the flames out, but they were spreading too rapidly.

Patel shouted, "I found the stairs!" She waved her flashlight so the rest of the group could spot her, through the billowing clouds of smoke, in the back of the front display area.

Up they all went to the second floor, which originally had been another display floor for customers.

"We have to get to the roof, before this place goes up like a torch," Mostyn said.

He and Patel went looking for a set of stairs and found them in the back room, where there were rusting sewing machines and rotting cutting tables. A large area of the floor showed water damage and part of the ceiling had fallen in.

Mostyn took the stairs and Patel waved her flashlight so the others could find her.

Up they went and came out on a landing on the third floor. There was a door and a ladder. Mostyn played his flashlight beam on the ceiling and saw that the ladder ended at a trap door.

"Hopefully that leads to the roof," he said.

He climbed up the ladder and pushed on the door. The rotten wood gave way and Mostyn poked his head up through the hole. The dark expanse of the roof was before him.

"Come on up! The air is nice and cold."

From down below, he heard Kemper say, "Great." He scrambled out onto the roof and in a moment the others had joined him.

The sky was free from clouds and the moon was a few days shy of full. Its ghostly white light was being blocked out by the billowing clouds of smoke from the floors below.

"Okay, people," Mostyn began, "we need to find a way off of this roof and onto the one next door. Start looking."

There was a yell, followed by Baker's cries for help. Patel's flashlight picked up his hands holding onto the edge of a portion of the roof that had fallen in. Mostyn, Kemper, and Patel rushed to the edge and grabbed hold of Baker's arms.

"We got you, Baker," Mostyn said. "Hold onto our arms."

He clasped Mostyn's and Kemper's arms and they began hauling him up until his camera strap got caught. Patel took out her knife and cut the strap. The camera fell to the floor below and Baker was hauled back up to the roof.

"Damn," he said. "I really liked that camera."

Kemper hit him. "Is that all you can say? Next time I'm stepping on your hands."

Baker laughed. "Sure, Dotty. You do that. And I'll never take pictures for you again."

"Whatever. If we don't get off of this roof, we're going to be roasted long pork."

"Then I suggest you quit yapping and get over to the next building," Mostyn said.

"We only have one choice," Kemper shot back, "you know the grocery store is only two stories and that means a one story drop to that roof."

"Well, Kemper, get moving," Mostyn said.

First Patel, followed by Baker, Kemper, and lastly Mostyn, jumped over to the next building to the south of the burning clothier.

This building too had part of the roof fallen in, leaving a gaping hole which revealed the building's interior.

Mostyn went to the alley side of the building and looked over the ledge. He found the fire escape, but part of it had rusted away and fallen to the alley below.

"The next building to the south is only half a story lower than this one and it has a slanted roof," Patel reported.

"Does it have a fire escape?" Mostyn asked.

"It does. But it doesn't reach the roof, sir."

Mostyn took a look for himself. He noticed a couple skylights, the glass having long ago disappeared.

"We might be able to get inside that building through those skylights," he told Patel.

"Good plan, sir."

Behind them, flames were now visible through the hole in the roof of the old clothier.

"Doesn't this place have a fire department?" Kemper asked.

"Thank God there's no wind," Baker added, "otherwise this entire block would be a raging inferno in no time."

A door opened and out shambled four men onto the roof. Mostyn and his group turned at the sound and immediately saw those bulging, unblinking eyes gleam in the moonlight. The ghostly light also reflected off the rifles and shotguns they were holding.

"Down," Mostyn yelled.

He and Patel dropped their flashlights and took out their pistols.

One of the men croaked, "Surrender."

However, before Mostyn could even reply, one of the others raised his rifle. Mostyn and Patel opened fire. In mere seconds all four of the Agate Bayers were down before they could get off a shot.

"Patel, get the others to that building."

"Yes, sir."

Mostyn went over to the fallen men. In the background, he heard Patel's voice directing Baker and Kemper. Before him were four men. Two were still breathing. He took their weapons and holstered his pistol. A motley assortment of two double-barreled shotguns, an old bolt action 30-06, probably an M1903 from the First World War, and an even older Sharps single-shot rifle.

He searched the men for ammunition and found a

dozen shotgun shells, two stripper clips for the 30-06, and four rounds for the old Sharps. He stuffed the ammunition into his pockets and hauled the weapons over to the edge of the building.

Noises were coming from the stairwell leading to the roof. He ran back and closed the door, then ran back to where the weapons had been piled.

"Kemper and Baker are on the next building, sir."

"Go, Patel. I think more are coming. Take this shotgun." He dug around in his pockets and produced the shotshells. "Take these."

She took the shells and went to the edge of the building, while he stretched out prone on the roof with the other shotgun in his hands.

When he heard Patel announce she was on the roof, he got up and made his way to the edge of the building. The door flew open and a gun fired, taking out a chunk of brick just to Mostyn's right. He whipped around and fired one barrel of the shotgun. The men tumbled back into the doorway. Mostyn aimed and fired the second barrel into the doorway.

"Patel, take these!" He dropped first the empty shotgun and then the M1903 into her hands. The Sharps, he slung across his back, and then lowered himself over the side of the building and dropped down onto the roof.

Above him he heard the horrible hoarse barking and spine-chilling croaking that apparently passed for some form of language amongst the Agate Bayers. It was, though, a sound Mostyn had never heard a human being make.

First one and then a second shotgun blast sounded in the night. Patel was down on one knee covering him.

"Come on, sir."

"Go!" Mostyn commanded.

Patel dropped through the glassless skylight, having dropped the other weapons through to Baker and Kemper while Mostyn was dropping down onto the roof.

Mostyn followed Patel, several bullets smacking into the roof around him.

In the excitement, he'd forgotten his flashlight. Patel, though, had hers and used it to illumine the room they were in, although the light didn't fill the room due to its size.

Kemper came back from a window. "There's a bunch of them in the alley. The fire is spreading, too."

Baker added, "I counted about a half-dozen out on the main street. It's not looking good for the home team."

"Don't get all down in the mouth, Baker," Mostyn said. "The fat lady isn't even on stage yet, let alone getting ready to sing."

"So what's the plan, Mostyn?" Kemper asked.

"You know how to use a shotgun, Baker?" Mostyn asked the photographer.

"I do. Just point and shoot. Like a camera, right?"

"That'll work. Patel give him the shotgun and the shells. Who wants the M1903?"

"I don't like rifles," Kemper said.

"I'll take the rifle, sir."

"Ever shoot one, Patel?"

"Yes, sir. M16."

"Right. Navy."

Mostyn passed the stripper clips to her and held out the other shotgun to Kemper. She shook her head. He held out his hand to Baker and Baker passed two shells to him.

"Okay, people, let's get down to the ground floor."

"Stairs are over here, sir," Patel said.

Down the stairs they went, Mostyn in the lead, having taken Patel's flashlight. The building was empty, cleaned out sometime in the distant past. On the main floor, Mostyn went first to the back door. It was made of wood and was hanging crooked on its hinges, the doorframe splintered where the bolts had been.

"Patel, you and Kemper create a diversion in the front. Hopefully, you can draw off some of the men in the alley. Once they're gone, we'll make our escape through the alley." He handed the flashlight back to her.

The two women went to the front of the building. Mostyn peeked out and looked up and down the alley. To the north, flames and smoke billowed out of the old clothier and smoke was pouring out of the buildings on either side. On the other end of the alley, blocking access to the street were several Agate Bayers.

Mostyn pulled his head back inside.

"What are our chances?" Baker asked.

"If we can get across the alley and cut through one of the buildings or take the fire escape up to the roof, I think we'll have a good chance to get out of here."

Gunfire sounded from the front of the building and in a moment Patel and Kemper came running into the backroom.

"They're making an assault!" Patel yelled.

"I guess we have no choice," Mostyn replied.

He dragged the door fully open, peered out into the alley, and dashed across, inciting a volley of gunfire. Baker pointed the shotgun down the alley, pulled a trigger and dashed across, firing the remaining barrel when he reached the other side to allow Kemper to cross.

Baker reloaded and Mostyn called out to Patel, "On three!" He counted to three, Baker fired one barrel of the shotgun, Patel dashed across, and then Baker fired the other barrel. A cry came from one of the Agate Bay men.

With Mostyn leading, in single file they sidled along the building wall until he found a door. Though locked, the rotten wood gave way on the first kick. Mostyn went in, with Kemper and Baker following.

The Agate Bayers were advancing up the alley. Patel dropped to one knee, squeezed the trigger on the rifle, worked the bolt, and squeezed the trigger again. The men scattered. She worked the bolt, stood, squeezed off another round, getting a cry of pain from one of the men for her effort, and joined the others inside the building.

Patel turned on her flashlight and the group walked through the abandoned building until they reached the front door. She turned off the flashlight. The moonlight gave the room an eerie glow.

The store looked to have been a five and dime many years ago. Now it was nothing more than rotting and decaying wreckage.

Mostyn crouched down and slowly opened the door. He crawled out onto the sidewalk. They were on Washington

Street, next to the liquor store which was now closed. Moonlight illuminated a large section of the street, which appeared vacant. He looked up and saw the glow of the fire behind them in the sky. He stood and signaled for the others to follow.

"For the moment, we're safe. Now we have to figure out how to leave this place."

"What about the way we came in?" Baker asked.

Mostyn shook his head. "If I were them, that's where I'd be watching."

"There must be another road out of town," Patel offered.

Mostyn nodded. "Probably. Again, though, if I were them I'd be watching there as well."

"What's that leave? A hike through the woods?" Kemper asked.

"That's one route," Mostyn replied. "We can also try the rail line. They might not think of that, since it's aban-doned. Or at least looked like it."

"So what will it be, Mostyn? North or south?" Kemper asked.

"Let's try the railroad," he replied. "Be easier than trying to find our way through the woods."

Keeping in the shadows of the buildings, Mostyn, followed by Baker, Kemper, and Patel, made his way down Washington in the direction of the lakeshore and the rail-road siding. He paused at the intersection of 4th Street long enough to let several shambling figures move down the street to the west. The fire over on Main was sending great clouds of smoke into the sky and the moon was no longer visible. The light from the flames reflected off the smoke and gave the night an eerie feeling, as though one was in the very bowels of hell.

When the shambling figures were out of sight, Mostyn and his team crossed the street and continued on their way.

At 3rd, there were more figures. Some seemed to be loping and others had a peculiar hopping motion to their gait. Mostyn watched one shadowy figure point and one of the party took off loping in the direction the other had indicated. When the rest of the party had turned a corner, Mostyn signaled for his team to cross the street. However, he hadn't gone far when he signaled a stop.

He pointed towards Lake Superior. Over the lake the moon was not obscured by smoke and fire and cast a pale luminosity upon the water. The group followed Mostyn's pointed hand.

Patel was the first to speak. "Oh, my God! What is that?"

"Looks like a lot of people swimming," Baker observed.

"I don't think those are people," Patel corrected. "No human moves the way they're moving."

"A trick of the moonlight," Kemper said.

"No," Mostyn replied. "You're right, Patel. Come on, we have to cut through the forest. No time to get to the railroad. And we need to get to the trees before those things get here."

Mostyn turned and began running back up Washington, his team following. The moon was sinking in the west and obscured by the smoke and spreading fire. The sky was aglow and yet the streets were mostly in the shadows due to the buildings obscuring the direct light. Nevertheless, Mostyn avoided the middle of the street and kept to the shadows cast by the buildings on the west side of Washington.

At the liquor store, Mostyn smashed the glass of the door, unlocked it, and entered. Baker, Kemper, and Patel followed him in.

"Patel, use your flashlight. We have to find a telephone." There was a hint of panic in Mostyn's voice.

She played the beam around and found the phone underneath the counter. It was an old-style one with a dial in the base, a mouthpiece on top of a slender pole, and the earpiece suspended from the switch hook. Mostyn took the receiver off the hook, put it to his ear, and then dialed a number.

"Special Agent in Charge Pierce Mostyn. ... zero-zero-eight-eight-zero-four-four. ... Code Twenty-one. Repeat. Code Twenty-one. Agate Bay, Minnesota."

He put the receiver on the switch hook and set the phone down. "Come on, let's go. Patel, you lead."

Down Washington they trotted. The fire over on Main looked to have spread to the entire east side of the street in the block containing the grocery store and the old clothier.

"If they don't do something about the fire," Kemper said, "the entire town is going to be burnt to ash."

"Not our problem," Mostyn replied. "Might even be a good thing. Come on. Quit dawdling."

"God, Mostyn. I'm not an Olympic sprinter."

At the intersection of Washington and 6th, as they

crossed the street, several shots rang out. The team dropped to the pavement.

Behind them, could be heard the horrible croaking and guttural jabbering of a massive throng. In the building kitty-corner to them, a hoarse voice rasped out the word "surrender". Kemper shouted back, "Go to hell!"

The fire seemed not to have crossed 6th. If they could make it across the intersection, they at least wouldn't have the fire to worry about.

Mostyn ripped out a clump of weeds from a crack in the pavement. He called out, "Patel, watch the corner. Shoot when you see the muzzle flashes."

"Yes, sir," she called back.

Mostyn tossed the clump of weeds. Three flashes and reports and a split second later Patel fired. Behind them was the raucous noise of the horde from the lake. He laid down the shotgun and took the Sharps off his back and dug out two rounds from his pocket. He took aim at the windows where the shooters were located.

"Low crawl," he called out, and the team members ahead of him began crawling across the pavement towards the nearest building.

Bullets whined overhead and smacked the pavement. Mostyn noted the position of the muzzle flashes. Two shooters was how he saw things.

He took aim as best he could in the flickering illumination of the fire off the smoke that was behind them.

Another muzzle flash, and Mostyn squeezed the trigger on the old rifle. It bucked and even though the report was loud it was lost in the cacophony of sound advancing up the street from the lake. The shooting stopped and Mostyn crawled the rest of the way across the intersection to join his comrades.

The advancing horde was a block or two away. In the reflected light from the burning buildings he watched their progress and for all their peculiar non-human loping, shambling, and hopping movements they were advancing quickly. The dull roar of their croaking, barking, and guttural grunts grated on Mostyn's ears.

"Move on and quickly," he said. "I'm going to see if I can't slow them down."

"I'll join you, sir."

"No, Patel, I—"

"No" was all she said and crouching low ran across the street. She got down into a prone position and after sighting in her target opened fire. Mostyn shook his head and did likewise. Within a minute they were both out of ammunition for the rifles. Mostyn looked longingly at the old antique and then set it down, waving for Patel to join him in moving out to join the others.

"There are a few of them that won't be enjoying the party, sir."

"That there are. Good shooting there, Navy."

"Thank you, sir."

Running, they caught up to Baker and Kemper in the next block. Baker had twisted his ankle stepping on something in the street and was hobbling along, slowing their progress.

"You two keep going," Mostyn said. "Get to the forest and keep going until you get to the highway. Understand?"

Kemper took a long look down the street. "God, what the hell are they?"

"The Deep Ones and their half-human offspring," Mostyn answered.

Kemper continued, "They must be some manner of missing link."

Mostyn waved his hand to indicate they needed to get moving and added, "Now is not the time for you to go all anthropological on me, Kemper, and they aren't a missing link to anything except for maybe hell. They are pure, unadulterated evil. Now get the hell out of here."

"That's crazy talk, Mostyn."

"How many of these missions have you been on?"

"Too damn—"

Patel screamed and pointed. "Oh, my God! What is that?"

Mostyn, Kemper, and Baker saw it coming around the corner. It was huge and it was indescribable terror in motion.

"Holy shit," Mostyn said, almost under his breath. "It's a shoggoth!"

10

THE GIANT, AMORPHOUS, ROILING BLOB OF MULTI-
eyed insanity slid around the corner with the ease of a
giant snail, only much, much faster. The words "Tekeli-li!
Tekeli-li!" greeted their ears.

"Come on!" Mostyn yelled. "We have to get out of here
and fast! Run! Run! I'll help Baker."

The others, however, didn't move. They were staring at
the horror that was the shoggoth and seemed glued to the
ground.

Mostyn shook the women. "Patel! Kemper! Run. Or
you're dead."

The women shook their heads as if coming out of a
trance and took off down the street.

"Come on, Willie Lee."

The photographer pointed."Wh-what?"

"It's a shoggoth. Now let's go!"

Mostyn put his arm around Baker and Baker put his
around Mostyn and they followed the women.

The howling, baying, and croaking mob had scented their quarry and were in hot pursuit. To make matters worse, sporadic gunfire began peppering Mostyn's team, slowing their progress. Patel ran back to Mostyn and Baker. Mostyn passed his shotgun to Baker and, together, Patel and Mostyn formed a chair with their arms for Baker and continued the race to the forest. Kemper joined them.

"What the hell? I told you to run."

"Oh, stuff it, Mostyn," Kemper said. To Baker, she said, "Give me those goddamn shotguns and get the hell out of here."

Baker surrendered weapons and ammunition. Mostyn, Patel, and Baker took off down the street. A door opened and before the creature could get out of the building, Kemper had turned and fired one of the shotgun barrels into the thing. Its weapon clattered down the short flight of steps to the sidewalk.

Kemper picked it up, turned on the advancing horde and shot into the mass of creatures until the weapon was empty. She then picked up the shotgun she'd fired and discharged the remaining barrel, reloaded, and fired again; continuing until the ammunition was gone. She picked up the remaining gun, shot both barrels and then tossed the gun down, and ran after Patel, Baker, and Mostyn.

They'd crossed 7th Street and were halfway to 8th when a shot rang out and Patel stumbled and fell with a grunt.

Dotty Kemper caught up to her companions, and seeing Patel said, "Ah, shit. As if things weren't bad enough already."

Another shot smacked the pavement inches from Kemper's feet. She whipped around and fired a double-tap at a figure in a window. The shadow fell back into the room.

"Dotty, you and Baker get to the forest. I'll take care of Patel."

Kemper hesitated and Mostyn yelled, "Go!"

They hobbled off and Mostyn turned his attention to Patel. The mob was getting closer. The thunderous sound of what had to be hundreds of flopping, hopping, crawling bodies was deafening in and of itself. Add to that the bestial babel of croaking, baying, and barking and the night was an inhuman cacophony of all the imagined and impossible to imagine horrors of hell. Not even, Bosch, Goya, Pickman, or Bacon could paint such monstrosities.

"Come on, Patel, I'll carry you."

"No, sir, leave me. It's bad. I'll hold them off—"

"Forget it. We don't leave anyone behind. Remember?"

"Yes, sir."

"Good. C'mon. They're getting too close and I don't want them for neighbors."

He got her on her feet and they hobbled towards the woods. But not fast enough. A thing, impossibly bestial in its abnormality, charged ahead of the mob. Mostyn heard it, turned, and fired his pistol into its face. The .45 caliber bullet blew out the back of the thing's head and it collapsed in a twitching, quivering heap.

Mostyn let go of Patel, got down on one knee and aimed for the robed thing with the tall tiara on its head. He squeezed the trigger and the thing fell back into the mob behind it and was quickly swallowed up in their advance. And towering over the sea of nightmarish things was the multi-eyed and tentacled abomination that was the shoggoth.

"Leave me, sir."

Mostyn ignored Patel's request and picked her up in a fireman's carry. Off he went as fast as he could run towards the dense woods, which were beyond the last row of houses on 8th Street. Kemper was there, her pistol at the ready, to provide cover for Mostyn and Patel.

The horde of things, too obscene for even hell to contain, swept on, and Mostyn knew they were gaining on him.

Kemper shouted and yelled for them to hurry.

He was close and ran as fast as he could, carrying his wounded teammate.

Kemper screamed, "Look out!" And began firing her pistol.

A tentacle looped around Mostyn's leg and he pitched forward onto the overgrown weeds that had once been the yard of a Victorian-style home. He lost hold of Patel and in that moment another tentacle grabbed her, jerking her high into the air.

Her screams joined the bleating, croaking, and barking tumult rending the night. Mostyn got to his feet. He joined Kemper shooting at the viscous agglutination of impious horror. The bullets seemed to have no effect and in a moment, the thing, never ceasing its cry of "Tekeli-li! Tekeli-li!, opened a hole in its body and dropped Patel into it. The hole disappeared and Patel was gone.

Kemper grabbed Mostyn's arm and dragged him across the unkempt lawn, past the dilapidated house and into the forest. The things plunged in right after them.

Mostyn yelled, "Up!" And he began climbing a tree. Kemper followed suit, firing her pistol into the face of an especially determined creature.

The two shimmied up their respective pine trees. Below them surged the seething and noxious horde, the overpowering stench of fish, making Mostyn gag, filled the air along with their horrid and inhuman voices.

Kemper called out, "Any hope of getting out of here?"

Mostyn fired his pistol at one of the things trying to climb his tree. It's face disintegrated and it fell, landing on top of its compatriots. Pistol empty, and with no more ammunition, he hurled it at another creature attempting to climb the tree. He pulled out his backup and fired it until it was empty.

"That was my last bullet," Mostyn informed Kemper.

"I'm out too. Both guns."

"I don't know if the cavalry will get here in time. These things have us up a tree and we've nowhere to go."

"Great. Goddamn bureaucracy. Not worth shit except when it comes to counting beans and even then they can't get it right." She threw one of her handguns at a thing trying to climb her tree and scored a hit. It fell back into the crowd.

"Where's Baker?"

"I told him I was helping you and he should get to the highway."

"Do you think he can with that ankle?"

"Probably. If these things don't decide to go after him."

"Hopefully he'll make it."

"Mostyn, if we don't get out of this, well, I just want you—"

"Save it, Kemper. We'll get out."

Suddenly the seething sea of unholiness on the forest floor began moving.

"Looks like they're leaving," Kemper said. "Maybe it's their bedtime."

"Ever the optimist, Dotty Kemper. Unfortunately, I don't think so. Look."

On the forest floor, oozing around and between the trees was the many-eyed agglutination of indescribable blasphemy and horror. Even in the darkness of the forest it was visible due to the yellowish glowing of its bulging, lidless eyes. Eyes that lacked pupil and iris.

At the base of Kemper's tree, the monstrosity took shape. A many tentacled orb, covered in eyes, with a gaping, putrescent maw.

"Oh, shit," Kemper said and shimmied further up her tree.

The shoggoth, already fifteen feet tall, stretched out a tentacle past Kemper, who was about forty feet up the pine, to block any further ascent.

She threw her remaining handgun at it. "Oh, God, Mostyn. This is it." And as a tentacle snaked out in her direction, she screamed and screamed.

In an act of desperation, Mostyn threw his pistol into the thing's gaping maw. A tentacle snaked out, wrapped itself around Mostyn's tree, and began shaking it. His feet slipped and he held on with his arms, legs whipping to and fro. With a loud crack, the pine trunk snapped, and Mostyn felt himself falling.

The last thing he heard was the whump whump of a Huey's rotor.

11

PIERCE MOSTYN SAT AT HIS DESK, DRINKING coffee, and reading his own report on the Agate Bay case for the umpteenth time. He'd re-read the other reports in the file innumerable times as well. He'd been back to work for a week. Agate Bay seemed a lifetime ago.

He leaned back in his chair, coffee mug in hand, and thought back to that horrible night in the little village on the north shore of Lake Superior. A night he'd just as soon forget, but knew he never would.

It was cases like Agate Bay where he longed for the permanent oblivion dementia or Alzheimer's would bring. He couldn't help but think they might be a mercy. Something a good God should hand out to give peace at the end of life.

A comprehensive report had not yet been written on the Agate Bay case. From reading all the separate reports he'd been able to piece together a fuller picture of what happened on that night.

Five weeks ago, the helicopters arrived just in time to stop the shoggoth from making Kemper a snack. The Deep Ones had scattered and fled back to the lake. The shoggoth, being a shapeshifting being, had escaped.

The OUP operatives took him and Kemper to a secret medical facility run by the OUP, where he woke up the following day. He'd suffered a concussion and three broken ribs in the fall. Mostyn remembered the doctor saying they'd found him on top of some hideous being. A hybrid of human, frog, and fish. The creature had probably died on impact and without a doubt had saved Mostyn's life. The being had been taken to a secret facility and dissected. Scientists were studying it.

Baker had been found on the highway, limping in the direction of Two Harbors. Aside from the twisted ankle, he'd suffered from exposure in the cold night, fatigue, and emotional distress. After a couple of weeks in the hospital, he was now at home.

Kemper was physically okay, but was suffering from Acute Stress Disorder due to the horrors she'd witnessed. Particularly that of the final moments with the shoggoth. The psychiatrists seemed to be of the opinion it was watching his fall from the tree that was the proverbial last straw. Seeing him disappear into that sea of living nightmares had sent her over the edge. She'd been found clinging to the tree screaming his name over and over. According to the reports, it had been with great difficulty that Bardon and the psychiatrists had gotten any information from her regarding that night in Agate Bay. She was sent home from the hospital a week ago and is currently on medical leave.

Bardon thought it best if Mostyn stayed away until she fully recovered. Mostyn smiled a bitter smile at that. After what she saw, no one would ever be able to fully recover. He knew that without a shadow of doubt.

Templeton, Patel, Caleb Peterson, and the grocery store couple had not been found by the OUP rescue team and were listed as missing in the reports. Mostyn, of course, knew Patel's fate. He could only guess at the fates of the others and was confident their bodies would never be found.

The OUP operatives had, with practiced precision, swept into the little village and rounded up over seventy of the inhabitants and had even succeeded in capturing eight of the monstrosities, which are now officially tagged as Unidentified Creatures, or UC for short.

The fire, before it was stopped, ended up destroying half the village. Over the past weeks the government moved in and erased Agate Bay from the map. Even Google maps shows the place as nothing but forest. All mention and record of the village is being put down the memory hole. The internet now has no mention of the place, at least the part ordinary people can access. Books will be more difficult to alter, but then not many read old musty volumes anymore. Perhaps that is an advantage. Maybe the digital age is in fact a wonderful thing.

The Coast Guard, in cooperation with the Navy, two weeks ago conducted training exercises off the shore of what was Agate Bay and Disaster Rock. Over three hundred depth charges were dropped into the deep water off the lake facing side of the Rock and over a hundred missiles were fired into the deepest part of Lake Superior.

Aside from the myriad of dead fish, Mostyn had no delusions about the supposed destruction of the Deep Ones and their city. Logically, given the amount of ordnance, they should have been destroyed. Unfortunately, the Deep Ones have a way of defying human logic.

There was a knock on his door. He sat up and set the coffee mug on his desk. "Come in."

The door opened and Doctor Bardon walked in. His short, pot-shaped pipe perfuming the air with the sweet smell of a Virginia blend. He closed the door and took a seat across the desk from Mostyn.

"Well, Pierce, my boy, how are you?" He pronounced the words in his precise and educated English accent.

"I'm fine, sir."

"Good. Good. Don't want my best agent out of commission for too long. Spoke with Doctor Kemper this morning by telephone. She seems to be doing quite well. I think Agate Bay has finally made a believer out of her."

Mostyn didn't say anything and Bardon went on. "Our new detainees will give us invaluable knowledge to add to the information the government got in Innsmouth. Science has made great strides since nineteen twenty-seven. We might actually be able to determine the origins of the Deep Ones. Too bad, though, we couldn't capture the shoggoth. Would have made a fine prize. A mighty fine prize."

Bardon had a smile on his face and a dreamy look in his eyes.

Mostyn let him enjoy his reverie for a few moments before clearing his throat and asking, "Have you ever seen a shoggoth, sir?"

The Director smiled and steepled his fingers. "Oh, yes. Oh, yes. Indescribably hideous things, aren't they?" He puffed on his pipe. "Antarctica. Nineteen sixty-five. Part of my doctoral research. Yes, indeed. No wonder Kemper got ASD, especially thinking the thing had gotten you. But then you know what it's like facing a shoggoth, don't you, my boy?"

"Yes, sir."

"Say, I'm very sorry about Special Agent Patel. She'll get a medal, of course, for her family's sake. Some nonsense about an operation in Yemen, or some such. Make them feel good that their daughter died a hero. We just can't tell the family the truth, now, can we?"

"No, sir."

"By all accounts a brave young woman and that's how she should be remembered."

"Yes, sir."

"We'll tell the same thing to Doctor Templeton's family. A brave search and rescue attempt, but unable to retrieve his body. A deep glacial crevasse or some such attempting to analyze bones or something on that order. I let the public relations folk do the creative work. I just sign off on it. And don't blame yourself, Pierce. You did the best you could in the situation with the information you had at hand. Devilish beings. Simply devilish."

Bardon stood. "Christmas in another week. Knowing

what we know, it gives a wholly different meaning to 'Peace on earth; goodwill towards men', doesn't it?"

"Yes, sir, it does."

"Again, I'm sorry about Patel. I know how you feel about a fellow comrade in arms, so to speak. If I don't see you before the big day, a happy Christmas to you, my boy."

The Director stuck out his hand and Mostyn moved around the desk to take it and they shook hands.

"Thank you, sir, and the same to you."

Bardon nodded at him and went to the door. With his hand on the knob, he paused, and turned back to look at Mostyn.

"Oh, before I forget, let Evelyn know where you want that Columbia Six delivered. Will you?"

"What? You mean...?"

Bardon chuckled. "I take care of my people, Pierce. Happy Christmas."

The director left and Mostyn returned to his chair. The Columbia Six. Just what he needed to take his mind off things.

"Nothing like restoring an antique," he said out loud, "to occupy one's mind. Just what the doctor ordered." He chuckled at the joke.

His mind's eye drifted back to the car and the garage and Templeton. At the thought of Templeton, the happiness faded away.

How could he not blame himself? He'd told the young anthropologist to wait with the SUV when he hadn't wanted to do so. No amount of antique restoring was going to erase that mistake. None.

He sat staring off into space and then got up and walked over to the window. Through the one-way transparent armor he looked at the day. The sky was gray and the temperature was below freezing. He thought of the jovial director and smiled at the comment Bardon had made and that he'd taken the effort to rescue the old car for him. Specially for him. Then his mood once more grew serious.

The tree outside his window was naked. The leaves long gone. Yet, despite the look to the contrary, he knew it was very much alive and for that reason liked to share his thoughts with it. He liked to think on some level it could hear him. Unlike the painted walls surrounding him. He liked to think nature was like that.

"I wonder," he said out loud, "how many families have been lied to because it wasn't expedient to tell them the truth? How many are we, the government of the United States of America, lying to right now? How many horrors are we hiding from the American people? Horrors, that perhaps they need to know about?"

Were those snowflakes dancing in the air? He couldn't be sure. The transparent armor wasn't quite as clear as glass.

"Peace on earth and goodwill towards men. I wonder if we'll ever see that." After a moment's reflection, he said, "Probably not."

He paused and thought of Dotty and what she had wanted to tell him that night and how he'd cut her off. "Why?" he said to the tree. "Why was I afraid to hear what she might have confessed thinking we were going to die?"

Out on the street a car drove by. Traffic was light this

afternoon. "No, we'll probably never have peace on earth. However, I can try to spread a little peace and goodwill on my own this Christmas season."

He walked over to the hat and coat stand in the corner of his office and grabbed his hat and coat. "Ready or not, Dotty Kemper, here I come. I think we both can use a friend and just a little bit of peace on this old earth and some goodwill, at least towards each other."

FROM ME TO YOU

I hope you enjoyed *Nightmare in Agate Bay*, the first book in the Pierce Mostyn Paranormal Investigations series.

If you did, please leave a review on the site where you bought the book, and on your favorite social media sites.

You review is word of mouth advertising, which is the best kind of advertising.

I encourage you to become a VIP Reader. You'll find out more about my writing adventures, get free and exclusive content, and other things of reading interest.

Click, tap, or scan the QR code to begin your adventure today!

CONTINUE THE ADVENTURE!

The OUP never sleeps. Dr. Bardon and his top agent, Pierce Mostyn are ever vigilant in saving us from the things that go bump in the night.

If you enjoyed *Nightmare in Agate Bay*, then continue the adventure with *Stairway to Hell*.

Mostyn and his team journey below ground to a hidden world of terror. A world from which there is no escape. Can Mostyn defy his captors and return to the surface of planet Earth?

Click, tap, or scan the QR code to find out today!

BOOKS BY CW HAWES

CW is a multi-genre author.

The books below are portals to his many exciting worlds. And no AI was used in the writing of these books. Books by a human for a human.

Pierce Mostyn Paranormal Investigations

The X-Files meets Cthulhu. Pierce Mostyn does battle with inter-dimensional monsters bent on the destruction of humanity.

Nightmare in Agate Bay
Stairway to Hell
Terror in the Shadows
Van Dyne's Vampires
The Medusa Ritual
Demons in the Dunes
Van Dyne's Zuvembies

In the Shadow of the Mountains of Madness

Justinia Wright Private Investigator Mysteries

Justinia Wright is the PI with panache. These slow burn mysteries, written in homage to Rex Stout's Nero Wolfe, are sure to satisfy your craving for intriguing puzzles, quirky characters, and wise-cracking humor.

Vampire House and Other Early Cases of Justinia Wright, PI
Festival of Death
Trio in Death-Sharp Minor
But Jesus Never Wept
The Conspiracy Game
A Nest of Spies
When Friends Must Die
Death Makes a House Call
To Right a Wrong
The Nine Deadly Dolls
Ripples on the Pond
Christmas with the Wrights
Minneapolis's Finest
Jack in the Box
Sauerkraut Days
Justinia Wright Private Investigator Omnibus Edition

Magnolia Bluff Crime Chronicles

Tense slow burn mysteries set in our favorite town in the Texas Hill Country.

Death Wears a Crimson Hat

Ten Million Ways to Die
Who Mourns Elektra?
Death by Moonlight

The Rocheport Saga

A post-apocalyptic adventure series in the style of cozy catastrophes such as *Earth Abides* and *Day of the Triffids*. Join Bill Arthur as he strives to build a new and better world on the ashes of the old.

The Morning Star
The Shining City
The Divided City
The Troubled City
By Leaps and Bounds
Freedom's Freehold
Take to the Sky

Decopunk

Alternative history adventures in a world where World War II never happened and swing is still king.

From the Files of Lady Dru Drummond
The Moscow Affair
The Golden Fleece Affair

Rand Hart Adventures
Rand Hart and the Pajama Putsch

Tales of the Macabre

For the horror lover in you.
Do One Thing For Me
Metamorphosis
What the Next Day Brings
Ancient History

Anthologies

Enjoy CW's stories in these short story collections.
The Phantom Games
Beyond the Sea
Overmorrow
Arachnapocalypse! The Anthology
Once Upon a WolfPack

Available at your favorite online retailer. Just click, tap, or scan the QR code to be taken to My Books page for buy links.

ABOUT CW HAWES

CW Hawes has written over 50 novels and shorter works of fiction. He was also an award-winning poet and had over 200 poems appear in ezines and and print.

He is a founding member of the Underground Authors and was the impetus for the highly successful Magnolia Bluff Crime Chronicles series.

After 35 years of working in county government, he retired at the beginning of 2015 and began a second career as a fictioneer. Perhaps some of the horrors Pierce Mostyn faces can be traced to his creator's own experiences in county government and beyond. Perhaps.

CW lives in Southern California. He enjoys reading, writing, chess and other board games, his daily morning walk, and contemplating the meaning of life while smoking his pipe. He also hasn't met a doughnut or a pizza he doesn't like, is something of a tea snob, and rocks out to Handel and Vaughan Williams.

You can get curated content and the occasional free story

when you join his mailing list, and you can reach him at his website, on X, and also Facebook.

To join his mailing list, click, tap, or scan the QR code:

To visit him on his website, click, tap, or scan the QR code:

To visit him on X, click, tap, or scan the QR code:

To visit him on Facebook, click, tap, or scan the QR code:

ACKNOWLEDGMENTS

No book is ever a solo project. There are all the folks who wrote the material an author draws upon for research. There are all the writers who are currently writing and who came before that the author has read. There are also all those who help on the technical end of things.

To name everyone who has helped me in the production of my books would be an impossible task. Consequently, for this book, I'm going to single out a few folks who helped make this book possible.

I want to thank Crispian Thurlborn for his kind words of encouragement and for producing the trailers to promote the book, a superb job that.

Thanks also goes to Ben Willoughby for his great cover.

Many thanks go to my beta readers who provided valuable input to make the story better. They were my sister, Jodi; my daughter, Susannah; Ben Willoughby; and Andy Decker.

A special acknowledgement must go to HP Lovecraft,

who's imagination and writing got the ball rolling in the first place.